Where Is Bear Going? written by Mark Janssen and illustrated by Suzanne Diederen

ISBN 978-1-60537-372-0

This book was printed in January 2018 at Wai Man Book Binding (China) Ltd. Flat A, 9/F.,
Phase 1, Kwun Tong Industrial Centre, 472-484 Kwun Tong Road, Kwun Tong, Kowloon, H.K.

First Edition
10 9 8 7 6 5 4 3 2 1

Written by Mark Janssen
Illustrated by Suzanne Diederen

Where Is Bear Going?

Clavis

NEW YORK

This is Bear.
He's taking a walk in the forest.
Where is Bear going?

"I'm going to see some sleepy little **eyes**!"

Look, it's Squirrel!
He's joining Bear on his walk.
Where are Bear and Squirrel going?

"We are going to see some cute little **ears**!"

On the way, they bump into Fox.
Fox is happy to follow along.
Where are Bear, Squirrel, and Fox going?

"We are going to see a little pink **nose**!"

Do you see Rabbit?
He's hopping along with his friends.
Where are Bear, Squirrel, Fox, and Rabbit going?

"We are going to see a teensy-weensy **mouth**!"

One, two, three, four . . . five!
Cat has joined in.
Where are Bear, Squirrel, Fox, Rabbit, and Cat going?

"We are going to see a soft little **belly**!"

Finally, they run into Goat.
He follows them with a big smile.
Where are Bear, Squirrel, Fox, Rabbit,
Cat, and Goat going?

"We are going to see Baby Mouse!
He was just born!"

Look! This is where Mouse lives.
Come on—let's go inside!

Look at Baby Mouse.
Isn't he sweet?
And look at those sleepy
little eyes, cute little **ears**,
little pink **nose**, teensy-weensy
mouth, and soft little **belly**.
Shhhh . . .
Baby Mouse is sleeping.

Bear, Squirrel, Fox, Rabbit,
Cat, and Goat all give him
a little kiss. "Welcome, Baby Mouse!
Can you come out and play with us soon?"